Find out more obout the author here!

A REASON TO SHINE

By Thea Eliss

High above the clouds,
where everything
glimmered and
sparkled,
Lived little Lucy, a
cheerful star who was
happy to shine.

One day Lucy found a lake, saw the reflection of the night sky and thought:

"I am just a star among thousands of other stars, some even bigger and brighter than me.

What difference does my light make?

Why should I shine?"

Lucy went to the moon to ask:
"Why should I shine if there are already so many stars?"

The moon replied:
"Every star has its **reasons to shine,** you only need to find **someone to shine for.**"

"One person?" wondered Lucy, "I can do that!"

Lucy left the sky to visit Earth to find someone she could shine for.

Lucy didn't know where to go, so she searched for bright things to see why they shined.

She found a brightly illuminated city and saw all the lights, small and big, that were there.

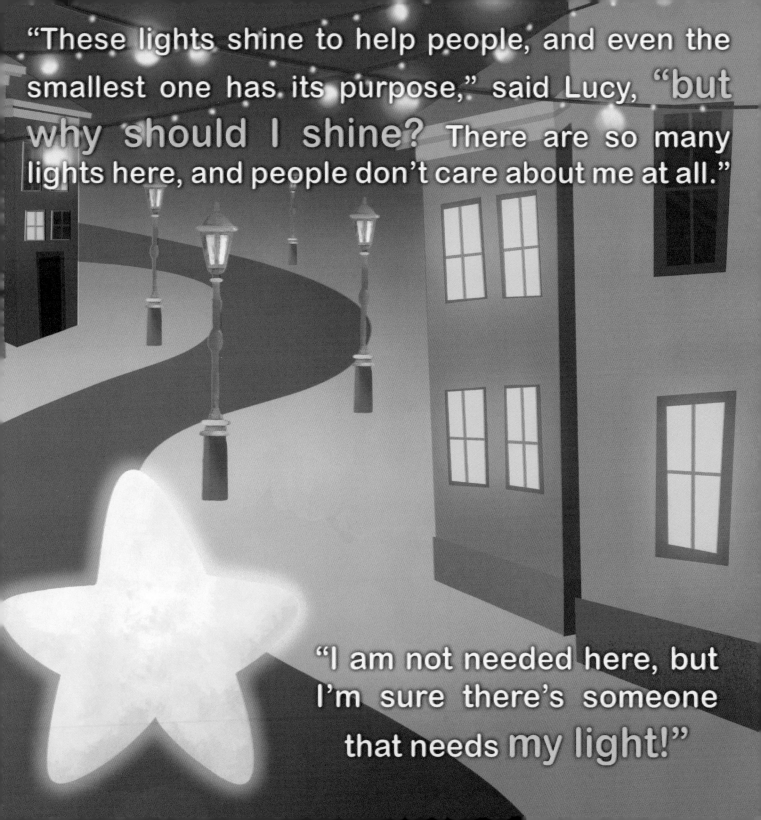

"These lights shine to help people, and even the smallest one has its purpose," said Lucy, "but why should I shine? There are so many lights here, and people don't care about me at all."

"I am not needed here, but I'm sure there's someone that needs my light!"

The sky was illuminated by fiery bright lights.

BANG!

BANG!

"Fireworks! Fireworks!" shouted the children from below. "They're so pretty."

"The fireworks have so many colors and <u>give</u> people happiness," whispered Lucy, "but why should I shine? There must be someone I can shine for, right?"

Lucy continued searching and found the northern lights. They filled the entire sky with their marvelous colors.

"The northern lights are wonderful," thought Lucy, "they captivate everyone that sees them so much that they forget about the stars. I can't compare, so why should I shine?"

Lucy started crying and floated away.

"There are so many lights besides the stars, and they all have a purpose. Nobody needs the light of a small star like me." Suddenly, Lucy heard voices whispering.

Lucy floated towards the place where the voices were coming from.

Behind the hill was a field full of flowers, but not just any flowers. They were **glowing** and in **full bloom**, even though it was night outside.

Lucy went to them, asking: "Can I help you? I could use my light to help you search if you lost some…"

The flowers interrupted Lucy.

"No, thank you, we don't need your help…"

"Of course not," whispered Lucy hopelessly.

"Because we've already found you!"
"Me?" asked Lucy, "I think you're
mistaking me for someone else."

"Nooo!" cried the flowers, "we could never mistake your light! It went missing some time ago and we got worried." "My light?", wondered Lucy, "but it's so small!"

The flower started telling Lucy how it couldn't bloom at first because it had a weak seed. It all changed when the light from a little star reached the seed.

The seed blossomed, and from that seed a field of flowers came to be, all thanks **to** the light of the star.

"That star was you, Lucy. It wasn't simply your light, but the warmth we could feel from it. There may be many lights in the sky, but none of them was your light! Even if it is small, it made a difference to me, to all of us!"

Lucy looked carefully around and saw that there were not only flowers, but insects and small woodland creatures as well.

"Not only did you help us," began another flower, "but you made us want to shine too!" "When we began shining, nothing happened at first, but then small insects started coming to us. They were too slow or hurt and could not find food during the day."

"It's because of us!" shouted <u>the</u> fireflies excitedly, flickering their tiny light! "We came and helped the insects find their way here, by guiding them."

"I've finally found someone that loves my light!" Lucy said proudly. She promised the flowers and animals that she would continue to shine and visit them sometimes.

Lucy was happy again, knowing that even the tiniest light, no matter how small or dim it is, could make the world a brighter place by finding its reason to shine.

THERE'S MORE TO DISCOVER!

Lucy loves animals! Can you find at least one animal in each page of the book?

HINT: look for constellations in the first part of the story!

Lucy needs your help to discover the hidden message of the story! Look for underlined words and put them in the spaces below:

_ _ _ _ _   _ _ _ _ _   _ _ _ _ _ _

_ _   _ _ _   _ _ _ _ _

Find **this**   Not **this**

ACKNOWLEDGEMENTS

Firstly, I would like to thank God for all the blessings I received and all that He's done for me.

I'm extremely grateful to my parents, my father who taught me to remain true to myself and my amazing mother from which I learned to love books and stories.

I am thankful for my incredible husband, who always believes in me and encourages me to grow.

I also wish to tank my wonderful brother and sister-in-law for always being there to lend a helping hand.

And last but not least, I would like to thank the readers for your trust and interest to read the story of a little star.

Dear Reader,

Thank you for reading the book. I hope you enjoyed my little story. Please leave a review, I appreciate any feedback! If you have any questions or comments, I'm happy to hear them all. Just send me a message at the E-Mail: **info@theaeliss.com**

Please visit my website:

www.theaeliss.com

to learn more about future projects and receive free materials for children.

Printed in Great Britain
by Amazon